The Road Trip 2

(Mother and Son's Secret)

Karena Donger

ISBN: 978-1-63750-298-3

Table of Contents

Content Warning

This book is solely for people who are over the age of legal adulthood due to its sexual content. There are themes with a lot of bad words. All characters are well over the age of eighteen.

Mom and I were exhausted as we came to terms with our post-orgasmic euphoria.

-- Joel

Free Bonus

Grab My "At The Beach (Erotic Romance Story)" Ebook For FREE!

Today you can grab your copy of my Free Erotic Romance story e-book titled – **At The Beach**. Best of all, it won't cost you a thing.

Download and Subscribe for Free book, giveaways, and new releases by **Karena Donger.**

Click the image above to **Download the Book**, and also Subscribe for Free books, giveaways, and new releases by me.

Or Follow the link below;

https://mayobook.com/karenadonger

As my subscriber, you will enjoy more free books exclusive to subscribers only, plus **Free Giveaways**. Wait no further, join my growing number of book lovers, and let's connect.

Road Trip Cont...

"Well, sweetie, there should be hot dogs here." What do you think? My Dad asked.

Is this a place where we can eat? What is the bus stop's name? Dad inquired as he parked the automobile.

"No problem honey... hot dog is excellent any time of the day... huh Joel?"

As she looked up at me, Mom tried to mask the dangerous, panting lilt in her voice by feigning a yawn and smiling.

As I thrust back, she was still sitting on my lap, rubbing her hefty, meaty ass against my crotch with my hands on her hips.

Mother: "Ugh... yeah?" I let out a groan. My dad might have misunderstood my gasp of pleasure as a positive response to her question.

As we resumed our dry humping, the only barriers

between us were her flimsy summer dress and panties and my shorts and boxers. I was trying to enjoy the ride as much as possible before we had to stop soon.

When it was 10 miles away, it was a completely different story.

Innocently enough, the day began.

Dad, Mom, and I finally finished packing our car to the brim with all of my belongings for college, which was five hours away on a scorching late August afternoon (nearing midday).

When I noticed at the last minute that my enormous flat-screen TV had been left out of the packing, I insisted on moving everything else to make room for it. When I insisted on bringing that electronic device, I didn't anticipate that it would lead to an all-day ride with my lovely, mature mom.

She had given birth to me (her only child) at the age of 19, and despite the passage of time, she still appeared to be in her prime. Mom had curly, shoulder-length, dark brown hair and wide, brown eyes with naturally long lashes.

She was small, perhaps 5 feet tall. She has a striking resemblance to *Martha Harper* from the television program **"Weeds,"** but in my opinion, she is more attractive and has a more appealing facial beauty.

Even a few hours ago, I wasn't thinking about these things because our journey had been delayed by Mom's insistence that we all take another shower before we left, and I was a little irritated by her. The day was hot, and we were all sweating from transporting and packing all of my belongings, so I didn't see the sense in continuing the conversation.

It was only when we were ready to go that I realized how cramped the front seat was, with my 42-inch TV occupying much of the space that Mom and I could fit.

Dad and I were the first to hop in. When he saw me, barely able to see above the TV, he inquired whether

Mom and I were okay (it was turned sideways with the screen facing my side of the car). The only thing that bothered her was whether or not Dad would be able to drive, so she crammed herself into my lap and insisted she was alright.

At last, we were on our way, and I found myself looking sideways in the rear-view mirror, saying my final goodbyes to the places I had called home for the previous 20 years.

I didn't notice her until we were on the road for about twenty minutes when she sat on my crotch with her smooth, naked legs brushing mine. As recently as a week ago, I was thinking about my ex-girlfriend, with whom I had broken up because she had decided that we should just part ways peacefully because she was moving to a different college. When I realized that this was my mother's warm, gorgeous butt pressing firmly on my penis and pent-up balls with only a few pieces of clothing in between, I felt conflicted about possibly never seeing her again and frustrated about not having had any pussy in the last few months.

To my horror, I was becoming a boner as a result of my repressed lust! My erection was responding to the unanticipated feminine stimulation produced by Mom's ass, so she must have felt the sprouting log of my erection.

I attempted to distract myself from the embarrassing situation by listening to the radio, but it didn't work.

My hands accidentally brushed against Mom's bare thighs as I became a little dizzy and couldn't find anything else to hold on to. I noticed that Mom's dress and skirt had ridden up as she started fidgeting a little.

At first, she just asked if I was okay, but as her writhing around on top of me became more rhythmic, I realized how much she must have been enjoying it.

She put her hands firmly on her thighs after grabbing mine. In the end, all I needed was consent from her to give in to nature's impulses, and that was given to me by her sly grin and the glazed expression in her eyes as she fluttered her lashes up at me. We were all dry humping!

From there, things only got better. *Even though we occasionally peeked over the TV at Dad as he drove to make absolutely sure he didn't notice what we were doing, we grew more daring in our prohibited amusements with time.*

When Mom invited me to finger her wet pussy when her pants were down to her knees, I was shocked. She started a conversation with my father about how long the trip was and how she was feeling. Mom's dress was unbuttoning and I was tickling her plump tits and having my way with her body while I agreed with him that we were good.

Even though we had another hour or so of driving ahead of us before we were likely to stop for lunch, I knew I had to push my big dick in Mom and fuck her as good as I can possibly do.

I had no idea if this opportunity would ever come my way again. A few feet away, Mom and Dad were engaged in a raunchy double-sided conversation, and I, too, was eager to join in, hoping to ratchet up the sexiness so that both of us would be able to satisfy our sexual desires.

She offered me the opportunity to liberate my aching big dick rapidly as she permitted me to make an excuse to swap positions. Her panties slipped from her knees to the floor when she elevated her ass just a tad too high. **JACKPOT!**

I swiftly dragged her back down as her hot, spread buttocks looked inviting. This time, I finally got her to allow me to enter her inviting tightness, but it took some time and further tweaks.

In one fast shove, I was able to easily slide my cockhead and veiny shaft inside Mom's damp, sticky vaginal. When I hit rock bottom, Mom let out a cute, horny groan (distractingly drowned out by the radio) and I smirked as she chatted with my ignorant Dad.

We were in a frenetic, tumultuous, taboo fuck, and Mom was an expert at disguising her words with double meaning. She even got me involved.

It was at this point that her words became too much for us both, and she screamed all over my big cock while I was burying myself to the balls in her and blasting her vagina full of cum. The force of my climax ejaculation had both of my legs frozen straight out. When I spastically jerked my legs, ropes of hot, healthy sperm were released into her vagina with each jerk. This made all of the anxiety and aggravation from the previous months and the previous weeks seem to go away.

Mum sat calmly while I drained 5 months' worth of rage into her – her hot ass squelching my whirling nuts.

With her twitch, she managed to coax every last ounce of passion from me. At one point, while the cum-shot continued to fire, I could feel her cervix lapping squarely against my cock tip.

Her most sacred spot, the place where babies are

born, was being invaded by thick white wads of my potent, youthful gunk, which contained my energetic genetic messengers.

My hot, 20-year-old cock made me understand my mother was still only 39 and could definitely still get pregnant, but at the time, I didn't give a fuck. Having a condom on hand was the last thing on my mind when I packed my bags today.

Hopefully, she was on the pill. Regardless, I'd fuck her again as soon as I could. Even a small part of me wished that I had knocked her unconscious. My small, little swimmers meeting her egg; our DNA combining; Mom conceiving and giving birth while I was away at college; then making Dad assist in raising my child, thinking it was his—it was all so dirty, perverted, and nasty!

I was disgusted! During the time Mom was on my chest, I wondered how big her clammy tits would get as I kneaded them with my fingers. That my cock milk could be directly responsible for her jugs producing milk made me chuckle.

Mom and I were exhausted as we came to terms with our post-orgasmic euphoria.

Mercifully, we hadn't made it to Dad's planned lunch break at the rest area when we put our clothes back on. While it was still a few miles away, Mom and I were able to get in a bit more fun. Before we stopped, my hard-on had returned, and I wanted to spend as much time as possible with her hot a** before it went away.

After Dad's abrupt question about the breakfast cafe, we were unable to continue our playful adventure any longer.

We arrived at the restaurant, and Mom and I were forced to put an end to our merrymaking. Before she sat down slowly on me, she lifted herself up a bit and quickly straightened out her skirt, perhaps so Dad wouldn't notice. Personally, I had to find some way of getting rid of the fresh hard-on in my shorts before we were allowed to step out of the vehicle. Mom flashed me a wink when she realized I was in trouble (in more ways than one) due to my erection.

"Uh... honey? Surely Joel can go back there and check on his belongings to see if anything has changed, don't you think? " She told my Dad.

"It's definitely a sport." Then he handed me the keys while he turned off the car's engine.

After both of them emerged, *I took a few moments to admire the view of her ass that had been riding me (and I'd been pounding her) for the last few hours.*

That hard thing wasn't going to go away easily, so I'm delighted Mom came up with this plan to help me calm down.

After what felt like an eternity, I was finally able to leave after only a few seconds. To pass the time, I feigned to tie my shoelaces and then kept reaching back and pretending to check on my other belongings.

Yes, my baby's favorite TV is OK. As soon as I got

outside, Mom began to torment me.

"Yes, Ma'am," I reply. I laughed and rolled my eyes back at her.

Her hair was being styled, and Dad was extending his legs next to her.

It's a wonderful concept, honey! Mom uttered the words, then lowered her head and reached for her feet.

Prior to the next two-hour ride on top of our young son, "*You gotta stretch while You can!*" Said my Dad.

My mom smiled sexily, fluttering her eyelids, and she giggled back.

Squats were not something she had ever done before, so she carefully bounced her large rear a couple times like she was doing them. Reluctantly, I turned away after realizing that this was doing more harm than good to my lower body.

I went to the back of the car and opened the hatch,

deliberately shifting a few items and stalling. Taking a pair of basketball shorts from a bag and slinging them over my shoulder, I headed out the door. In high school, I used to have one of these, and I remembered how well the breathable mesh fabric worked for me when I was on a state-qualifying team. Wickedly, I wondered if it would be useful in the future for a few other things. I guess you understand what I mean. *Wink*

I've got to go pee now. Keep in mind that we still have at least two and a half to three hours of driving ahead of us. With that, Dad stormed inside the restaurant like a bull.

My mother walked up to me slowly after making sure he was no longer there.

She smooched me sexily as she snatched her purse from the trunk, noting my basketball shorts.

"Well, sort of?" *"But seriously, Mom, it's freaking hot out here,"* I said meekly. Simply put, I want something *"cooler."*

She slapped my butt as she giggled, saying, *"Something easier to get off like it right?"*

In the words of my Mom, *"Joel, you are a silly boy!"*

When Mom called me by my name, I assumed something had gone horribly wrong, but the light-hearted tone in her voice as she laughed made me feel better.

To ensure our safety, Mom hopped in the car to kiss me in the middle of the back seat with her tiptoed heel.

You were *"extremely bad"* for fiddling with your mother in such a way, but Mom liked it! As she cooed, she nibbled my lobe and kissed me on the cheek.

She gasped and collapsed into my arms as I yanked her closer to me with lusty jerks.

You're not allowed to be out here, young man! She reprimanded me in a mocking manner, her finger pointing at me.

Joel, hurry up and have your slacks changed. We still have a long way to go, just like your father said. "

My increasing bulging penis was gently caressed, with her emphasis on the term *"looooong"* as she did so.

Mom, if you don't leave me alone, I'll never be able to get comfortable! No worries, I'll smack you in between now.

As I bent down to reach inside her skirt and fondled her juicy pussy, stressing *"I'll be right in there..."*

When I tried to get closer to Mom's slit, she quickly twisted away, smacking my palm away in amusement.

What a scoundrel of a son! She said, *"What would you like Mommy to get for you?"*

Whatever my dad is eating is fine with me. The final time, I held Mom by the waist and said, *"... like maybe his wife!"* She nodded in agreement.

I gave her a cheeky squeeze through her skirt, then sent her out with a final slap of her rump.

As we parted ways, we both gave each other a philandering smile.

In my basketball shorts (which were both cooler and less restricting), I headed to the restaurant to get some food.

As was their tradition, Mom and Dad sat across from one another and chatted happily as they ate their "breakfast for supper."

Finally! Take action now, Joel. When we served you pancakes, we weren't sure if you wanted anything extra, so we prepared a plate for you. *"Here, have a seat beside me!"*

We both sat down, and Mom patted the seat in front of us. She only had bread, a little salad, and some fruit and juice on her plate.

Besides the pancakes, bacon, and sausage, he also had a cup of coffee. My father, who is approaching

50 and has a receding hairline, needs to pay more attention to what he eats.

Mom, this is fine. All of that fried food is out of the question for me. For the coach's tryouts next month, I need to keep my basketball shape.

It's not important, so don't worry about it. " As a matter of fact, honey, a young person requires a lot of carbohydrates. He'll have to haul all that stuff afterward, you know, young man! Dad slapped his son's leg with an irritating cackle.

Even if I wanted to smirk or "accidentally" kick him in the shins right then and there, I couldn't help myself.

Joel, don't listen to your father. She reached under the table and secretly pinched my nuts through my shorts while saying this without anybody else in the dining room knowing what she was doing. Her actions made it difficult not to groan.

I'm really sorry. I forgot to bring my basketballs with

me.

"Mom, would it be okay if you brought them over next week?"

"Of course, my son."

Just hold on to them till then, okay? Mom smiled as she massaged my balls under the table.

Upon my arrival to join them in the diner, I wondered,

"So, what were you two talking about when I arrived?" As I tucked into my pancakes," I inquired.

After getting back on the road, I was ready to eat the dinner so I could serve it up to Fucking Mom once again.

"Oh, no worries, I'll be back in no time!" *"...and visit you!"* was a risky pause.

You know, assist you with settling into your residence hall. She said to me.

"Next weekend would be ideal," I said.

Mom's gorgeous brown lashes fluttered as she smiled at me.

When Mom blinked her clandestine invitation for more incestuous sex, it was as if we were using a secret telegraphic code.

I can't wait to see you, Mom, next week! I'd definitely appreciate your help in unloading...

"In order to give her time to digest that period of silence, I purposefully popped some pancakes into my mouth. Meanwhile, I was fantasizing about fucking Mom's brains out all next weekend and unloading my balls on her. Unloading my belongings and organizing them was what I'm talking about openly, as opposed to what my real plans were in my mind."

Grinning back at her, I returned the lusty stare that had been exchanged between us without words. We were lost in thought.

"September is the busiest month of the year for my job, and I can't join you and your mother on the trip because I'll be too busy at work," Dad interjected.

You're welcome, Dad. In my dorm, Mom and I will be fine. (Fine while we fuck freely!) I sneered at my own thoughts.

Mom was the first to finish her light dinner and make her way to the women's bathroom to "freshen up," whatever that meant.

Having eaten most of what was in front of me, I was eager to resume our journey, but Dad was taking his sweet time.

When Mom came out of the bathroom, he was chewing on a toothpick and had finished his meal. There was something strange about her, but I couldn't place what it was at the time (later pun intended).

Do you think one plate of pancakes was sufficient for you, sportsman?

"Is there anything more we should buy for the trip? The sun will fall soon, and we're only halfway to your school, so I don't want to stop for food again," Dad said.

As soon as he got outside, he lit up a foul-smelling cigar.

The answer is *"yes,"* I said.

Don't pretend that you won't get hungry after a few hours. It's got to be the youthful vigor and metabolism, right?

"Go with your father to the car; I'll place another order with the waitress for more food." Mom hurriedly closed the little purse after retrieving her wallet.

With a *"whatever,"* I shook my head and made my way out the door.

"Come over Joel!" So; I did a brief twirl and returned to her.

"Be a sweetheart and put Mommy's purse back in the trunk," she instructed. She dragged me back when I

was about to leave the room.

"If you take the time to look around, you may be in for a pleasant surprise," she said, her voice hushed.

That grabbed my interest.

After one last tug, she peered up into my eyes and then down at my crotch suggestively.

When I get back, I want to make sure you're all *"settled in,"* she mewed, one of her fingers just touching the waistband of my shorts, pulling at it a little.

I dashed outside to our car as fast as I could, more so to avoid popping a boner in the middle of that diner in front of everyone's eyes.

So; when I went to put Mom's purse away in the trunk, I immediately snapped the lid off to see what "surprise" she had in store for me.

What I witnessed had me in a state of awe -- In the purse she had been carrying around, white cotton pants were found. She was completely bare naked beneath her summer dress at this moment. Upon closer inspection, I discovered a wet spot in the crotch caused by our mixed juices—her cream and my seed—leaking from her cunt.

In the blink of an eye, I had a hardon.

A few minutes later, it dawned on me what Mom's subtle change in demeanor was...

It wouldn't be long before I was putting more than just my fingers on that! That's more like my fat crotch!

I returned to my seat at the back of the car and waited impatiently for Dad to finish smoking his cigar and for Mom to return. It's possible the cigar could be a blessing in disguise; it might mask some of the odors.

I nervously pushed my fingers into my waistband and lowered my basketball shorts to my ankles, remembering Mom's earlier order to "*settle*" myself in. No one outside could see this eager 20-year-old sitting in the back seat of our car with a rude erection tenting high and tall from his crotch because of our car's tinted side windows.

After finishing his cigar, Dad got in the car and heated it up. No doubt about it, the smell of the cigar would mask some of the odors. After what seemed like an eternity, Mom emerged with a white paper bag containing the food.

"Oh!" As she opened the door to the car, Mom said something to me. She rapidly handed the bag to me and slipped back into my lap before anyone else could see her.

"The two of you can get settled in, but let me know when you're ready to go." As he fumbled with the wipers and headlights, Dad said. (He had no idea of what was happening.)

I adjusted the seat backwards to make a little more room for the bag. She grabbed her short skirt's hem as I lifted her up by her thighs. My hands followed hers and subsequently rested atop hers as I lowered her bare ass onto my throbbing cock in slow motion.

Both of us sighed with pleasure as my hard, naked dick made contact with her smooth, soft behind for the second time in a row. Fortunately, the radio was back on, and Dad didn't hear a peep.

After a few squirms of her cute little butt, Mom allowed me to get a good grip of her delicious rear end with my veiny shaft.

"We're good to go now, dear... The sun will set soon, and you know how terrible your eyesight is in the dark. Don't hurry to reach our destination. "

That part of my life is still ahead of me, you know. Dad took a deep breath and huffed.

Remember, we've got all the time in the world, dear... "Just remember, dear..." Mom paused, then went silent.

Finally, we were on our way again as dusk fell, the sun beginning to set over our heads in the west as we made our way through the countryside. As Mom writhed forward and backward on top of me, my raging erection still rubbed against the crack in her hot, bubbly ass. It wasn't until a few miles into the ride that I realized how much I was missing out on the pleasurable sensation of the rubbing between my shaft and Mom's butt.

When she got into it, she really got into it, thrusting her wide hips up and down, with each upward thrust, my engorged member rising ever higher. In the end, I shifted slightly on one of her up-thrusts and fissured it astoundingly along the lips of her slowly creaming wet pussy as my dick approached heaven.

As Mom's slick slash slathered my cock with the first layer of her honeydew, we both let out a soft, breathy moan. Oh, how I want to re-enter her cozy confines and plow her under once more!

Even though I was out of her pussy, my mother kept me entertained by gently stroking the length of my shaft with her fingers, peeking into my privates to check on how much sweat had collected on the top of my sperm-filled balls, and stroking my cock's head as she purred softly in my ear. Her sweet, tight pussy was all I could think about, and I couldn't wait to scoop it up and unload another thick stack into her womb.

Even as the minutes and miles ticked by, Mom's taunts managed to keep me at bay. But don't get me wrong, I was greatly entertained by her eroticism.

She was driving me crazy! A long time had passed, yet Mom's enticing words had eluded my achy tool for all that time. If I didn't pounce on her as we both knew she needed, would she just let me go?

After leaving the dinner, the fact that no one had spoken to us since then made us uneasy, aside from the radio music. Damn it! That wasn't an option for me.

"How long are you going to keep torturing me?" I whispered in her ear.

Her grin spread across her face as she replied,

"You've got to show me you're hungry enough, Joel."

What on earth did you mean by that?

Mom handed me the bag of food from the restaurant as if she had read my thoughts because she reached down and casually picked it up. I was still perplexed as to what she was trying to say. Looking inside, I couldn't figure out why I was so perplexed. In addition to some bread, there were several Styrofoam containers with large sausages, scrambled eggs in one, and a container of some white stuff — probably gravy. I handed the bag back to Mom because I didn't understand why it was so important to me. Exasperatedly, she rolled her eyes at me.

You're starving, aren't you, Joel?

It was shocking to hear a normal-volume voice after so many miles of silence (*aside from Mom and my whispered messages to her*). It appeared as if Mom was overstating her voice.

"Yes, of course, Mom. What's in there, then?"

I went along with it, even though I had no idea what was going on. We were continuing grinding, but suddenly it stopped when Mom raised her ass to get up, and then made a point of audibly rummaging through the paper bag.

What am I going to do?

"I've got these buns. They look great, don't they?" I asked her, with a childlike tone of voice.

As she returned with the dinner rolls, she gave them to me with a smile. Despite my confusion, I held them up to my face and looked at them. A few seconds ago, I was about to bite into one.

What do you think of these BUNS, Joel? Mom went over it again and again.

My attention switched from the bread to the obvious wriggling inches in front of me that I had missed. What the hell is going on?

Her skirt was cinched at the waist, exposing her ass while her hips moved sensually back and forth.

When she spread her buns apart, she did it with both hands on her buttocks.

Those hairs! The realization of it all came to me more like a flash of lightning.

Mom, you're right. *"Then I'll get a taste of that! "*

"That's OK, son. Dive right in! "

It was with my hands on her hips that I brought her down hard to my crotch. My mother extended a helping hand and lifted my stiff cock to meet her gaze. Touchdown! with a single horny thrust. My mother's clammy, pussy-clutching lips were punctured by my cockhead and shaft, and I was completely submerged in her cunt.

After she was snugly nestled in my balls, I slowly raised her up and lowered her slowly back down. After that, it was time for some more ball-busting fun, and I was in heaven!

The best buns you've ever had, Mom! *Mmmmmrrrgh...* Grumbling, I pretended to be eating.

That's right, son. I'm aware of the situation. You'd like some more of this?

Smacking her lips, Mom replied.

My shaft was soon covered in Mom's juices as we sped up. To further enjoy the tightness of her succulent pussy, I squeezed her hips even tighter. Her ample butt was just the right height for me to eagerly thrust up into, and our pacing and timing were perfect. I could feel my hard cock back in heaven.

"Ha! Are you two still peckish? I knew you should have stuffed yourself at the dinner. Maybe I should stop driving for you both to stretch a bit?"

When he interrupted our filthy fuck, Dad's voice was loud and grating.

No, please don't! My mom said.

Joel, *"are you sure you don't want to stop?"* Her voice was a little shaky.

"No..."

My Mom said, we've got a long way to go... We can manage to stretch and readjust ourselves in the car. We don't need to stop until we get to the school."

That's all right, you two. Then carry on.

Honey, *"please don't make a mess in the car with you and your son about hunger! " My dad said*

We smiled at each other as we looked at each other. When she clambered forward, she drew out the container with the sausages and set it down on the counter. I was the first to reach for a fork and take a bite.

Mom, *"What about a bit of my sausage? "*

Mmmm...

Put it on my thighs, Joel! Your sausage is a lot more robust than the wrinkly one your father used to eat! " (She whispered to my ears).

"Mom, I know!"

We exchanged passionate kisses as we smacked our lips together. Then I really started giving it to her. Double-talking and putting one over on Dad were taken to a whole new level in this charade, and I was savoring every moment of it.

The pussy-lip-smacking and the constant "schluck! schluck! schluck!" of our unhurried and joyful forbidden fucking carried on for what seemed like an eternity, our false eating sensations helping to disguise the actual cause.

We didn't eat any of the pretend food because it was too gross, but I have to confess that the calories from the food did assist Mom and I continue our casual, illegal encounters.

The Eagles' *Witchy Woman* was screaming on the radio. Mom whispered in my ear as we were about 30 minutes from my college.

"It's time for you to take the final course."

The following container was pulled from my purse

by my hand. We kept up our feigned suckling. My cock kept on banging Mom's pussy from the bottom.

It's time for some more of that, son! My mother's whine was loud and desperate.

My genitals did as she asked and stepped up the tempo. It became more obvious that I would not be able to withstand the growing pains of my rumbling balls.

Your son, dear, is disobeying. "Tell him to give some eggs to his mother! " Mom told Dad.

"Pay attention to what Mom says, sportsman." Dad said.

"Are you absolutely certain, Dad?" I asked Dad.

"Danggit! Your mother will appreciate some scrambled eggs from you, son."

"That's fine, Papa!"

Suddenly, I accelerated my thrust to an ecstatic rate. As we neared our climax, Mom kept up with me, bouncing her plump, moist ass, meeting me stroke for stroke. The words I wanted to scream were ringing out in my head as I sat inches from my father:

"All right, Dad!" I'll cook Mom's egg for her. Her egg should be scrambled with MY SEED!!

What if I mixed her genes with my own?

THERE'S A BABY IN HER!!! I'M CREATING A CHILD IN HER!!! Those youthful, loaded balls will be shot dry of sperm before I put a baby up for adoption. Your dear wife, my mom! "**"

As soon as I felt the usual tingle and pang in my heavy, clenched nuts, I knew I had to take action. I could already tell this was going to be a heavy load when I got this close!

Joel, that's so good! That sack's bottom could be a little too far for you, son. "

"Yeah, Mom!" exclaimed Mom.

" *Mom?"* I blurted out. My mind was racing.

You can count on me to go deep into my nutsack for

you, Mom!

*You can count on me to go deep into my nutsack for you, Mom! 'That includes reaching deep inside of YOU! Millions of my Joel will be shot directly into your belly if you let me reach deep within you! If I can't go deep inside you and knock you up with my f*cking baby, DAD has NO IDEA HOW TO STOP IT!!! "** (Joel whispered)*

When I retrieved the container of white gravy, I chuckled once more at Mom's cleverness. There was nothing she hadn't considered.

"Mom, what are you going to do with this white stuff?"

"Joel, just get rid of it. I'd want some of that white, hot gravy on my eggs! Give me as much as you can!"

It's fine, Mom!

So that was it. It took Mom's final comments to pique my lustful curiosity about everything's obscene double meaning.

Then, with one final frenzied thrust, I was back in Mom's clutching cunt, my balls deep in the dirt. Mom's cervix was brutally penetrated by my pre-cum leaking cockhead as the first searing string of semen shot from my piss-hole in a single second. Staggering amounts of baby-batter, all of which came straight to Mom, down her womb.

"Uuuuuuuuuuuuuuuuuuuuuuuuuuuuu, Joel, you're leaking it all over the place! " Mom shrieked with delight.

That's certainly what I was thinking. My seed was strewn all over my mother. embedded in her were mounds of my ancestry. Even though I was exhausted, I continued going. Young adult sperm streamed into Mom's unprotected, receptive, and welcoming womb, one wad at a time.

Sorry, Mom, it's just so much! But, oh my gosh, it's so good, huh? " It made me want to throw up, and I moaned.

I made noises as if I was sucking my fingers, but what I was actually doing was sucking on one of Mom's firm nipples.

Mom was cuddling with me, and I realized it when I felt something warm dripping over my genitals. As I continued to push myself into her creaming fuckwit, her pussy would squirt her own delightful, feminine honey all over my penis. Stirring our raging stew of sexy, steamy, and hormone-fueled sludge, I bit into my lip and stirred. A bubbling brew was made when my mother and I mixed our banned, FAMILIAL Fuck-froth.

You are stirring it up so much! "Oh.. Joel, you are stirring it so much!!!"

"Danggit! It's awful, right? " Dad just kind of spewed it out.

"Nnnnngh... The majority of your son's white material got into my container, dear..."

You don't have to worry, Dad! Mom's package contained all of my gravy! "

There is no harm in giving your mother a second helping

if she's still hungry.

Mmmmmmm, ahhhhhhhh, that's fine.

"Yes," Joel, "Gimme some more of that gravy, sweetheart!"

'There you have it, *Mommmmmm!*'

Mom and I sighed softly after a full dinner as we indulged our primitive needs while also obediently honoring Dad's stupid instruction.

With the help of her pussy, my mother was able to extract every last drop from my genitals. I could feel Mom's squirming cervix slurping up my sperm like it was her own, and I was mortified. All of my possessions were eagerly given to her. As much of my swarming, swimming genetic gunk as I could get into Mom, in her hallowed womb, where kids are conceived, was my goal for this mission in life.

In order to discover her egg for as long as I could, I would send every last thrashing packet of DNA that my testicles could produce out into the world. It would be nice if Mom's ovaries helped out. The one thing I longed for more than anything else was the chance for one of my lucky baby-makers *(out of the countless millions I was giving Mom right then and there)* to meet Mom's ovum. Mother Nature would take care of the rest, ensuring that Mom would be knocked up in the process.

If he's done, make sure you acquire all of his belongings! I told you not to mess up, son! "

Don't worry, sweetheart! I've got it all covered. "

"Dad, I couldn't have done it!" I laughed cruelly to myself as I smiled.

Relishing in the sweet satisfaction of post-orgasmic adrenaline and youthful testosterone, my body was tingling with excitement. When I realized that I had once again crammed Mom's fridge to the brim, I felt like I had won the lottery.

As a bonus, I had the illicit thrill of knowing that Mom had been my consenting partner, knowingly putting one of my 20-year-old sperm inside of her 39-year-old Mommy eggs to meet. The prospect of becoming incestuously pregnant by me, her own son, seemed to excite her to no end. This all happened just inches away from her husband, my dad, who was completely unaware (or ignorant) of it all!

As we neared the college town's outskirts, I finally popped my satisfied penis out of Mom's ravished cunt. While peering into Mom's crotch, I was pleasantly surprised to find a minimal amount of slobber. The majority of my ammo must have been fired into her at the precise location I had in mind.

Despite the fact that Mom's skirt drooped down to her knees, she quickly straightened her skirt and pulled her thighs together. Smiling softly, she put her feet on the foot mat while crossing her calves and falling into me. My heart warmed when my eyes met hers and she smiled back at me. After that, I had peace of mind knowing my awesome deposit was secure!

My arms were wrapped around Mom's abdomen as I sat back and relaxed. I smiled wryly at seeing Mom raised on her elbows. Now that she'd provided them with some gravitational assistance, I wondered how my squirming mass of teenager-sized larvae were doing in her twat. After a while of lying like that, Mom got up and started cleaning off some of the crumbs and other debris that had accumulated in the back seat. My semi-hard cannon was a little unhappy to be put away as I put my basketball shorts back on.

My mom slid the window down, allowing us to breathe in some cool, refreshing late-summer air. We were both relieved when the thin film of post-fuck sweat that had been covering us vanished. Something else, of course, was scattered to the winds. I realize now that most of the car's lingering odor was caused by Dad's stinky cigar.

We got to my dorm just before 7 p.m. When we arrived, Mom was the first to get out of the car and dashed to the trunk to find her pants. Dad and I had just finished stretching when I noticed her dash to the restroom (I grinned to myself, knowing the true reason why).

After Mom returned, we began loading up my belongings, starting with my big-screen TV, which had been the source of my day-long fling with her earlier in the day.

When my belongings were finally unloaded from the car and delivered to my room, it was far past 9 p.m. As a result, I felt confident that I would still be able to spend the weekend with Mom alone.

The three of us made it back to the car together.

"Oh my gosh, how time flies by! My beautiful baby will be sorely missed."

As we prepared to say goodbye, Mom squealed and cradled me in her arms.

"Don't worry, my dear. Someday, they'll all have to leave

the nest and grow. And don't forget that you'll see him again next weekend to assist him with unloading. " My father comforted her.

Make sure to pack his basketballs, too, honey. Perhaps you and your mother could play a game of basketball next week, eh? "

"Hmmmmm... I'm stumped, my dear! A one-on-one meeting between your boy and his mother would be a good test. " Mom made a sly remark.

"Ah! I'm sure he'd shoot you all over the place! " Dad snorted and laughed.

My mother and I exchanged a sly grin.

My heart was full of joy as she came back to me and said, *"I love you."*

How about a little *"sport"*, or should I say *"young stud"*?

"Are you interested in continuing your father's wager? Mommy's basket with her other balls might be more fun,

though!"

I couldn't help but smile.

Mom returned to Dad's side, tugging on his arm with her free hand.

Do you think we might be able to have another child in the future? You DO realize how young I am? "

Ah! then What in the world did you come up with? As soon as our first child starts college, you're already talking about having another one! Besides, do you still take security measures? "

While Dad was shaking my hand firmly to say goodbye, Mom had a wicked grin on her face. She then returned my hypnotic glance.

As soon as I saw it, I recognized it.

"No, dear, I haven't been taking the pill for a while now."

The End

Check out the third book in this series Our Secret (Mother and Son's Secret 3) to read about how Joel fantasy grew bigger by fucking his mom, and also his aunt.

Thank You!

Free Bonus

Grab My "At The Beach (Erotic Romance Story)" Ebook For FREE!

Today you can grab your copy of my Free Erotic Romance story e-book titled – **At The Beach**. Best of all, it won't cost you a thing.

Download and Subscribe for Free book, giveaways, and new releases by **Karena Donger.**

Click the image above to **Download the Book**, and also Subscribe for Free books, giveaways, and new releases by me.

Or Follow the link below;

https://mayobook.com/karenadonger

As my subscriber, you will enjoy more free books exclusive to subscribers only, plus **Free Giveaways**. Wait no further, join my growing number of book lovers, and let's connect.

About The Author

I'm a romance writer and I've been writing for 10+ years. I write dark and romantic erotica. I have a penchant for romance. I also have a fondness for writing stories that inspire, and a love for the genre of romantic fiction. I write dark and erotic romance because I love the power of darkness and the eroticism that comes with it. I love the passion and the desire. I love the way a man will stop at nothing to get what he wants.

I also write fantasy and contemporary romance because I love the magic and adventure of it, coupled with the modern world and the characters in it. I love the modern family and modern relationships.

I have always loved reading romance novels, and now I am writing them too. I hope to share my love of romance with readers through my writing.

Visit https://mayobook.com/karenadonger to download my Free Erotic story **"At The Beach"** Today!

Other Books

1. The Road Trip (Mother and Son's Secret Book 1)

2. The Road Trip 2 (Mother and Son's Secret Book 2)

3. Our Secret (Mother and Son's Secret Book 3)

4. Our Secret 2 (Mother and Son's Secret Book 4)

5. The Road Trip Secret, Complete Series Box Set (Mother and Son's Secret)

www.ingramcontent.com/pod-product-compliance
Lightning Source LLC
Chambersburg PA
CBHW060601100726
47907CB00005B/1471